OPENING
THE
GATE

Short Stories and Poetry

By Wes Rehberg

Opening the Gate: Short Stories & Poetry
© 2012 Wes Rehberg
All Rights Reserved
Published by Wild Clearing
ISBN 13: 978-0615641201 (Wild Clearing)
ISBN 10: 0615641202

To Eileen
and to the survivors

ABOUT OPENING THE GATE ...

I was a newspaper journalist decades ago, wrote well-enough to pursue enterprise and even a few investigative stories, to brainstorm, guide and edit others' articles as well. But that experience is a great distance from what I'm trying now -- writing fiction, poetry, and nonfiction in short-story form. Inside this book are five short stories and five poems. Two of the poems have been published in a literary journal, The Rusty Nail. The writing within is the work of a brazen white-haired neophyte, an effort that I hope engages a piece of the soul and the mind of a reader and conveys the spirit of the content I had in mind when I set out to put into words what's within. May this be the case.
 -- Wes Rehberg

CONTENTS

THE SHORT STORIES

THE ENDURING

Cedric Malcolm drove his rust-colored pickup over the broken asphalt at the bottom of the hill, the camper in the truckbed rocking the vehicle from side to side. The asphalt gave way to a mix of gravel and dirt in a rutted series of steep upward bends. Wet days, like this one, it was gravel and mud.

"Damn," Malcolm swore, steering wheel jerking his hands as the truck pitched and yawed and strained with the camper's weight.

He had just retrieved the pickup camper from the edge of cleared woodland off another rural road where he worked with a logging operation, just after he was released two years ago from the New York maximum security prison in Elmira where he spent 11 years convicted of manslaughter in the death of his brother. It was his home until a year ago when he negotiated a deal with two elderly sisters his age for a vacant single-wide mobile home on this road, Claw Valley Pike. The logging operation ceased since then, the land was sold, and the new owner wanted the camper removed.

First time up this hill, he almost passed the aged small frame house on the right where the reputedly ornery sisters lived, obscure behind the beech trees, the evergreens, the thick brush, even in winter when foliage was gone. Across the way, a swamp nested where ducks once dwelled. No more. Muck and mire took over, with still enough seeping water from a spring for tadpoles in the ditch alongside the road, for cattails on its edge. When weather warmed, Malcolm could hear the awakening peepers at dusk and into the night, shrill waves of sound. Winter it would be coyotes and owls, and the occasional shriek of their prey.

At the hilltop, in the entryway to the rutted drive that led to the sisters' house, a rusted white mailbox leaned backward, likely shoved in that direction by a snowplow. Beyond, Claw Valley Pike narrowed downhill to a tight two lanes, When lumber trucks roared through, Malcolm pulled over to the side away from the ditch into the blackberry brush that lined the road. He'd tap the peak of his ball cap, greeting the drivers. They'd wave back.

"Bastard," he'd mouth with a grin.

Under the mailbox hung a faded wood sign that said Perkins. Perkins, Malcolm now knew, stood for sisters Ella and Marie, and more recently, for their tall, gangly and somewhat backward and very troubled nephew, Elijah. The sisters, usually ferociously protective and obstinately private, took in Elijah reluctantly when their brother Sam and his wife Margaret unexpectedly left town. The couple, owners of the single-wide Malcolm occupied, dropped Elijah off as they always did on Sunday on their way to the Crossroads Community Church of the Redeemer, about 5 miles away on old Route 71. Ella told Malcom the story when he negotiated lodging in the single-wide.

"'Y'all doin' OK here?' Sam asked me then" Ella said. "'Can I get you anything from the grocery.'"

"I said, 'I think we've got what we need, Sam, Don't be gone long.' I had no idea they were taking off."

"The two never showed up at church. Two days later, I filed a missing persons report, which led to a search for my brother's truck. They could identify it by a sign on the doors that said Perkins Contracting."

"Not that Sam did much independent work contractors do - his business skills weren't all that reliable," Ella told Malcolm. "He generally worked for other contractors or helped in logging operations around here."

"Two weeks later, border police reported they crossed at Niagara Falls into Canada, destination Alberta," she said.

Ella had then reached for a key to the single-wide, hanging on a nail on the rough-milled kitchen wndow frame. She put it into Malcolm's palm and smiled. Malcolm's hands were as heavily calloused as hers. She liked that.

"Margaret didn't really want to leave Claw Valley, or Elijah with us - we never really were friendly," she contnued. "And, as me and Marie worried, who knew what Elijah might do when he found out she and Sam abandoned him."

"Of course we had to take him in."

The other sister, Marie, later told Malcolm "He makes me uneasy, rocking back and forth and talking to himself like he does. He seems to be everywhere."

"For now, we put him in the attic room," Marie said.. "We had to turn the heat on,"

The sisters, both wiry and wily, inherited the house when their parents, Jason and Melba Perkins, were killed one winter in driving sleet and snow when their antiquated Ford station wagon slid off Old Route 71 into the frigid Susquehanna River. They had moved to Claw Valley when Jason had enough of coal-mining across the border in Pennsylvania. It was a new life for them.

They built their house and Jason worked as a tanner in a factory in Johnson City. To add income, Melba raised chickens and turkeys for the sale of eggs and meat. Ella was their oldest, then Sam, then Marie, all in their teens when the accident happened. Ella was adult age 18 so she took over the household, found a job in the local grocery store, and worked there until she retired seven years ago.

"We're going to just do it," she said after their parents died. "Nobody's going to put you two in a foster home."

The other two also worked odd jobs, so they were able to keep the house. Then brother Sam left when he and Margaret married. The couple took over the used trailer his parents had lived in when they first arrived in Claw Valley.

Ella managed things more than Marie in the sisters lives together afterward though both sisters learned quickly how to shoot and skin game and how to survive in the rawness of the woodlands. Ella took care of the household accounts, did most of the cooking, the negotiation with outsiders including the lumbermen for income -- she was always careful with lumbermen, no clear-cutting on their land.

Malcolm especially liked Ella, respected her grit, enjoyed the fire he felt in her, was amused by the way she would peer at him over her glasses with a book that always seemed to be in her hands when she wasn't working.

"You read much?" she once asked Malcolm.

"Only the no-hunting signs," he answered. "Just to ignore them."

Marie, who felt she was more fond of Malcolm than Ella, did the laundry and cleaned up around, but mostly she watched the soaps and read romance magazines. Both tended the garden as well as the the chickens and turkeys, but stopped with the fowl recently when it became too burdensome. Over the years they had grown to be a compatible, tough, independent twosome, yoked to the house in which they were raised, fierce in how they protected themselves and their land, even to the point of using a shotgun if needed. Neither had married nor wanted to. This was their domestic arrangement. People in the region learned over time not to mess with them.

And though Margaret did let Ella run most things, less work for her, she kept her voice in the decisions they shared. Elijah particularly disturbed her, she offered repeatedly.

"We aren't able to handle him is my opinion," she told her sister. "Somethings going on inside that isn't good."

"What else would you do?" Ella said. "Leave him to the wolves?"

Ella and Marie had two frequent visitors, one a Meals on Wheels volunteer who brought them and Elijah enough meals and nonperishable goods for a week, if they stretched it out. The visit had become a touchy moment for Karen Carter, the volunteer. The two barking chained up dogs didn't bother her but

Elijah did, leering at her, rocking from side-to-side, invariably in front of a woodpile when she arrived, a maul over his shoulders. He was almost always splitting wood when she came, outside so she couldn't avoid his presence. He also had a habit of toying with a shovel He twirled it, slapped it against his palms, tapped his boots with it, and hid his face behind its blade, then looked at her with a grin.

"Don't worry about him, Miss Karen," Ella said, a 20-gauge shotgun beside her rocker on the porch where it was usually when she was seated there. Marie also sat with a shotgun, double-barreled. "Nothing's going to happen here that a little birdshot can't cure. If it gets to that point."

"Just leave the boxes right there, on the stump. Elijah will pick them up when you're gone." she said, voicing a new arrangement to compensate for Elijah's presence. Carter usually brought them into the house.

Small comfort, Carter thought. Still, she felt obligated, and admitted to herself she felt intrigued by the challenge the visit now posed and the defining anxiety that came with it. She was also armed on her rural rounds in this northern nook of Appalachia with a 9 mm Taurus pistol for which she had a permit to carry concealed. She knew how to use it. Slim, short cropped pepper-and-salt hair, still a dancer, divorced, a bit of a carouser even at 53, she felt she still had the touch.

The other frequent visitor was Cedric Malcolm, his capped head shaved, bulky and muscular, shorter than the sisters, with a wisp of a beard,. They let him continue to occupy the single-wide after his job ended as long as he would once in awhile provide them with venison he'd deerjack or pickled small game he'd trap, as well as a case of beer, and worked for them a little.

They knew Malcolm had a history of rough living and served 11 years in prison, convicted of manslaughter in the accidental beating death of his older brother, Corey. They liked his toughness and his habit of saying what he meant. He could be trusted, they decided.

Malcolm never talked about the episode that led to his conviction, though he would swear to himself he could see Corey in the woods sometimes, watching him. The night of his brother's death, the two had fought in a bar across the border in Warren, Pennsylvania, Tink's Tavern, along the edge of the Susquehanna River. Cedric smashed a beer bottle across Corey's forehead and shoved him through the bar's glass window, Corey's carotid artery cut by the glass. He died too fast for anyone to help.

Because he was a felon, Cedric Malcolm couldn't own a gun, so he'd borrow one of the sisters' shotguns for his hunts. They also kept the supply of deer slugs he was still able to buy. Venison was more scarce these days, though. Wildlife personnel microchipped some deer to track them. Malcolm had to be careful.

"What you got for us today?" the sisters would ritually ask on his visits.

"You girls like muskrat, pickled muskrat?" he answered on his last trip. "Goes good with Miller Light."

"Done right, it's OK," Marie answered coyly.

"County mountie was here today," Ella teased. "He check in on you?"

"You know that," he replied. "You'd think I was still on parole."

"Trooper rode by yesterday," Ella said. "You catch that?"

"I might have gone into the grocery," he said and winked, motioning he head toward the woodlands.

"Whatcha got in that pack," Marie laughed, pointing to the V where his legs joined his hips.

"Nothing that you'll ever see," he'd smile back.

Especially with Elijah there. They were sure he'd be listening, or even try to peer in from the outside to try to watch. Ella kept their father's old .44 revolver near her bedside at night, which she was still strong enough to shoot, and Marie locked trigger blocks on both shotguns in her room, the key on a bracelet on her wrist when the sisters didn't have them at their side.

Elijah, usually brooding and restless, knew his aunts protective ways. He figured he also could get around the sisters if he had to. Some things you just know, he thought to himself.

Though he barely could read and dropped out of school at age 16, hating the special education classes he had to endure, he wasn't that dumb, he thought. Tall and powerfully built, lanky like his aunts, he had physically thrashed more than one boy who teased him in school. Even when three jumped him one day when the schoolbus dropped him off at the single-wide, he handled it. They broke his nose, but he had hospitalized one of the boys, a concussion from the rock he used, and broke the ribs of another with his fists. The third locked himself in the car the boys arrived in. Elijah then kicked at the door, the sole of his foot first, and dented it.

The schoolbus driver called the police, and his father Sam, equally as big as Elijah, seized him from behind, held him across his ribs, pinned his arms, and backed both of them against the trailer until Elijah calmed down. Sam and Margaret Perkins often would say they had had enough with him. He had tantrums at home, broke things, still he never tried to hurt them. But how long would that last? Something inside him was unhinged, ready to let loose.

Elijah took special care to behave himself with his aunts, to restrain whatever it was that made him want to destroy things. He felt protective, productive, respected, even though he saw they were wary. Things were always hard to understand, to cope with. The month he spent in a juvenile institution from the schoolbus incident didn't help his temperament either. The others there were worse than the boys at school, though after a couple of run-ins, they mostly kept clear. Elijah also had a deep suspicion of "outsiders from outside," he'd call them, people that were strangers to the area he lived in. The intrusions unsettled him to the core. Were they coming for him, like when he was brought him to the "juvie"? He never felt secure and could flare up unexpectedly so the sisters kept things as mild as they could. Now a little less able to handle their own survival, they began to let him do some of the heavy work. Elijah knew his limits with them. It helped. To a point.

With winter nearing, Elijah occupied himself with the woodpile, often supplied by Malcolm, easily handling the maul, sing-songing a string of thoughts while splitting logs.

"Chop, chop, the chopping block. Mock me, sucker, I'll crack your rock. No way, no way, you'll get away. Chop, chop, the chopping block."

He'd also unchain the dogs, pick up the shovel he liked to toy with, and daily walk with them in the woods, feeling as if he set them free, himself free, connected to something along the trails and long-abandoned logging roads that would settle him.

"Free, free, run for the sun. Dogs are gunning it on the hunt. This way, that way, anyway now. Free, free run for the sun." He kept time by tapping the shovel against his palms.

It wasn't entirely unexpected, a day in that looming winter that etched itself in Malcolm's mind as another defining moment in his life. It had a particular eerie vibration that chilled him, that he could feel sweeping across the ancient outcroppings of tree-covered bluestone shale like a wild spirit in the wind, something you knew that was part of the woodlands, hills, streams, ridges and hollows of the region. Still it seemed sudden, the sisters sensing it too, electric. They looked up at the sky, dark gray clouds moving much more swiftly than the gray mass above them. Heralds of foreboding.

Both the sisters and Malcolm heard the vehicle coming up Claw Valley Pike, the tires in the loose gravel and dirt, coming from the direction of the Pennsylvania border.

"Damn this road," said Randolph Edwards to himself as he checked the time on his dashboard clock. One more visit and then I'm off for three days; the afternoon hadn't gone well, he thought, unsettled and impatient. The week hadn't either.

Edwards negotiated his Forester four-wheel drive around the long lumber truck parked to one side on the dirt road. He was a landman, a go-between for the enterprise he was part of, Ecoproxy LLC, and one of the major oil companies that drilled in Pennylvania for natural gas in the huge Marcellus Shale deposit that stretched from West Virginia into New York. For some he encountered, the deep horizontal hydrofracture drilling process brought deadly pollutants into peoples lives and the environment. Resistance was highly organized. For others, "fracking" meant jobs and a flow of leasing money for farmers and others afflicted by a very depressed economic climate. Coalitions were formed among landowners to protect their interests and help them obtain a better deal than the big fuel corporations offered.

Edwards' job on his rounds was to persuade land owners to ignore both the coalitions and the environmental concerns and broker a separate deal through Ecoproxy for surface and mineral rights leases. A pipeline was already in place in the county and transfer stations were built to help move the Pennsylvania gas to another newly built pipeline that traversed the area. New Yorkers needed to hurry to be part of this, was his pitch. But he wasn't the only landman in the region; others were trolling landowners for competing brokers and drillers.

Edwards stopped at the single-wide Cedric Malcolm occupied and was advised that Malcolm could make no deal, it wasn't his land.

"Not you, then who," he asked.

Malcolm declined to answer. But Edwards had a good idea from the county GIS tax map he obtained. He asked whether there might be someone home where the Perkins sisters lived.

"Take your chances if you want," Malcom said. "But I'd be ignoring that place if I were you."

"We'll see," Edwards said. He brushed off the warning. Damn the obstinacy of those in this rural region, he thought.

He was tired, impatient and annoyed. Bad day, bad week, he had to try once more to make a deal. He pulled into the sisters driveway, glanced at the no-trespassing sign, decided to ignore it, and drove up to the yard in front of their house. The sisters had been expecting Karen Carter and the weekly supply of meals and, though they heard his vehicle, they were surprised to see it nearing their porch. Marie felt to her side for her double-barreled.

"What have we got here," she said to herself.

Dogs barking brought Elijah from behind the woodpile where sat on a stool feeling energy and restraint flowing through his head and body in rhythmic slow eruptions. He was there, excited and agitated, because Karen Carter was due to arrive.

Elijah put down his maul and picked up his shovel and waited. This ain't Karen, he thought, seeing Edward's car. Who the fuck was it anyway. He felt angry. It was, as he put it, an "outsider from the outside." They're always trouble.

Ella stood up and walked to the porch steps.

"You can't read the sign?," she said loudly, hand on one hip, as Edwards slid out of the car with a brochure and papers in his hand. She descended the porch steps, looked at his eyes, and figured he'd come to con them. He'd be condescending as well, she thought.

"I'd like to show you how you can make a lot of money," Edwards said.

He glanced over to Elijah, who started to slap the back of the shovel blade against his left palm, chanting something Edwards could barely make out, rocking from side to side. What is this, Edwards thought? He listened as best he could.

"Slap, slap, what you want, Jack? Looks like a stray from far away. Say, say you wanna play? Slap, slap, I'm tracking you, Jack?"

I don't like this, Edwards thought.

"You didn't answer my sister's question," Marie said. She stood up with her shotgun. "Didn't that sign mean anything to you?"

"I don't mean to impose, really, but I thought you might be interested in what I can do for you. Get you up to $1,000 an acre for the use of a small piece of that acreage. How many acres do you have here?" He knew the answer from the tax map: 240.

"I'm sure you could use it."

The sisters looked at each other.

"Damned if it isn't a landman," Marie said.

Edwards, now unsettled, thought it might be better to leave. Behind him another car entered the drive, approached his and stopped. It was Karen Carter, as expected. He was blocked.

"Damned if it isn't, Marie," said Ella. "The woods seem thick with them these days."

Elijah stepped closer to Edwards' car, the slaps of the shovel against his palm louder.

Ella turned to Elijah and signaled him to keep away. Carter looked at the scene, put her pistol inside her parka, eased out of the front seat, walked to the back of her Ford Escape, and drew out a heavy brown carton with the weekly meals. She walked around Edwards toward the porch, Elijah's eyes following her. He was between her and the stump where she usually placed the meals since his stay with the sisters.

"Just wait a second, Miss Karen," Marie said.

"You know," said Ella to Edwards, "I'm really getting ticked off at the way you landmen think you can just come to any old place out here and try to sell us a bill of goods. The coalition is almost as bad, thinking they need us to strengthen their hand negotiating with likes of you and the big shots you represent, people who would turn their property into sewers. But you're the worst."

"Just a second," Edwards responded, glancing between the sisters and Elija. With Carter standing near, he thought he could advance to the porch to show them the brochure. This is an act to scare me off, he decided. He stepped toward Ella. Marie raised the shotgun. Carter backed up a couple of steps and put the box on the ground, between her and Elijah. This definitely doesn't look good, Carter thought.

"Look," Edwards said, resuming his movement to the porch. "Just let me show ..."

Marie, the least patient of the two sisters, pointed the shotgun upward and pulled the trigger of one of the barrels. The blast startled Edwards and Carter and the dogs. Elijah became further agitated.

"Mr. Landman. You weren't invited to move this way," Marie said.

Elijah mimicked what Marie said, stepped to Edwards' vehicle, slapped his palms harder with the shovel, then tapped the hood with it. This man arrived at the wrong time, he thought. Now I'm going to make it the right time. He felt gleeful.

"What the hell do you think you're doing," Edwards said to Elijah, not moving, frightened.. Elijah cocked his head and tapped the windshield.

"I'm fucking with you, man. I'm fucking with you," he said. "I'd like to fuck with her, too," he said, ginning at Carter. "But my sisters wouldn't like that. But you ... ?"

Elijah felt pleased with himself.

"I'm a man with a plan and a shovel in my hand," He put the shovel blade up to his face, looked at Edwards from behind it for effect, then tapped the windshield. "Landman, landman, look where you landed. Right in the middle of my mess, I guess."

Just then, Cedric Malcolm rode up the drive and parked close behind Carter's car. At the same time, Carter reached into her parka and put her right hand on her pistol.

Malcolm exited his truck, took in the scene quickly, decided to play it light, entering what he felt was a ring of disturbance he knew too well. He figured Edwards would ignore his warning.

"Y'all are having a party here, I see. Am I invited?" He strode around Carter's vehicle, nudged her, looked over at Edwards, spat, and walked to the porch.

"I see the pretty meal on wheels arrived, too, And you, landman, you forget what I told you down there?"

No, this wasn't the time for light-hearted jibing. He changed his tone.

"This landman was just by me," Malcolm told the sisters, nodding in Edwards direction. "I didn't send him up here. Just want you to know that."

"You stay right where you are," Marie said.

"Elijah, get away from that vehicle," Ella followed.

"Not this time," Elijah said softly. He modified his chant:

"I'm a man with a plan and a shovel in my hand. Landman, landman, look where you landed. Right in the middle of this mess, hell yes. Can't run away now, we gonna play."

With his head tilted upward, lanky muscles tensed, Elijah stood for what seemed like a long moment. He felt as if he was as tall as the trees. He growled, lifted the shovel high and slammed the back of it into the windshield, sending forth a sharp metallic shattering sound.

"I like that," he said forcefully, and hit it again and again. The glass rippled in spidery circles. Edwards bolted toward him, Elijah saw this, whirled, swung the shovel at Edwards' head, and hit him in the ear. Edwards rocked to the side and looked at Elijah, stunned.

Totally unexpected, he thought, intermittent lights strobing in his eyes. Totally unexpected.

Marie reacted, pulled the trigger again, fired into the air, the second shell in her doubled-barrel shotgun now gone.

"Elijah!," she shouted. "Back off!"

Carter backed around the stump, her pistol now in both her hands, pointed at Elijah. No, this most certainly does not look good, she thought. Malcolm, meanwhile, lowered himself, hunched down, hands on his thighs. He was used to brawls. Let's see where this goes.

Elijah had trouble containing himself, he knew that from therapy. At the same time he seemed freer inside then he'd ever been. Deep within, resentment churned. Yet he felt joy, a contradiction he couldn't fathom. It didn't matter. He lunged toward Edwards, stopped to watch him dart backward, grinned at him, lunged again, watched again, then gushed a hoarse laugh and rammed the shovel into Edwards' rib cage, knocking him to the ground. Then he raised the shovel again.

"Elijah!," yelled Ella, now with her own shotgun raised "What in god's name are you doing. Put that down, get over by the woodpile! You hear!"

"Woodpile, my ass," he said, feeling calm, at the same time shuddering. He turned in Karen Carter's direction, feeling things were going to be completed, shovel over his shoulder. "Not without this one."

Carter straightened her arms, and aimed her pistol.

"Back away, Elijah," she said. "I don't want to do this."

"No way," he said.

Carter pulled the trigger and shot Elijah in the right shoulder almost point blank. The shovel fell from his hand and he reeled backward as Malcolm sprinted, lunged, and tackled him at the waist. Both landed on the ground and rolled over each other into the brush. Elijah broke away ferociously, jumped to his feet, and feeling completely at a loss, lifted his unwounded arm to the sky and let out piercing repeated howls, left palm faced upward..

The howls, coyote-like, carried through the woodlands, echoed through the foothills of the Catskills nearby, alerted the ears of wildlife. One could have sworn it shook the smaller trees, made the evergreens hiss, cracked the thin coatings of ice on rainwater that still puddled in the shade.

It was a tableau that a caustic primitive country artist could have painted -- Marie placing two more birdshot shells into her weapon's barrels. Ella with her own pump shotgun sideways across her torso, controlled. Edwards, on his side, propped on one elbow, right hand on his bloodied head, dizzy, coughing, trying to sort out his thoughts, numb, his left side ribs broken, the shovel blow blunted by his insulated vest. Carter with her pistol still pointed at Elijah, steady, alert like she'd never felt before, heart pumping. Malcolm on his knees ready to spring again if needed, youthful with the adrenalin rush. And Elijah, one armed raised, shouting at the sky.

Red Jessup had just finished his sandwich, drank a little hot tea from his thermos, and slumped down in the passenger seat of his rig connected to the lumber trailer he parked on the dirt and gravel hill, loaded with hemlock. He planned to nap a little when he heard the first shotgun blast, then the second, then the pistol shot.

This is different, he thought. He moved behind the wheel of the cab, started the truck, eased it up Claw Valley Pike toward the sisters' place and parked it in front of the drive, air brakes wheezing. He took his cell phone from its carrier on the rig's dashboard, lowered himself from the cab, and tapped the numbers 9-1-1 on the phone, thumb on the call button. Just in case.

Elijah howls were now breathy when Jessup walked along the driveway. The scene before him prompted him to complete the call.

He had known the sisters for as long as he drove the lumber truck through the backroads of these hills, how many years now. He knew that they were feisty -

tough, he would say, very tough ladies - and that they were not afraid to defend themselves, felt fierce about that, But he had never known anything this extreme to happen with them. This was new.

Jessup ignored Elijah, walked over to Malcolm, and with their hands clasped, raised him to his feet. He knew Malcolm well and was aware of his efforts to give the sisters a hand, even if some of it wasn't exactly legal. Malcolm always seemed to know where Jessup hauled away trees stripped of limbs and would drive there with his truck to pick up firewood, most of it for the sisters' woodpile. The hired-on woodcutters would help Malcolm load even as they loaded their own trucks, understanding the destination of the shorn limbs. A respect passed among them, though they'd tease him about being "a kept man."

Jessup turned from Malcolm to Karen Carter and suggested she lower the pistol. She said, "Not yet." She also knew Jessup. He once invited her into his cab. She declined.

The gazes of Marie and Ella met Jessup's and the three nodded, neither woman changing her stance. He then bent over Edwards, examined him, and told Malcolm to get his first aid kit from his rig.

"It's behind the front seat," he said.

"What about Elijah," Malcolm said, pointing in his direction. Elijah faced away from the tableau, now silent. Pain throbbed in his shoulder and down his limp arm. Jessup shook his head no. "Too hot to touch."

Elijah heard his name, turned, looked at them distractedly, the scene a haze, turned away, felt the blood ooze from the front and back of his shoulder, and walked to the woodpile, where he slumped down on a stool. He sat for a moment, then stood erect, stabilized himself and headed into the woods. The others watched him move away; it was just too much. The dogs, silent throughout the action, wanted to follow, as if this was the routine.

Sirens were heard in the distance. A phone rang inside the sisters' house.

Ella looked at her sister, cocked her head as if to say, keep an eye on this, stepped through the wooden door, picked up the receiver, and waited for a sound. She didn't recognize the caller ID.

"Ella, this is Sam. You there?" Ella didn't answer. What timing, she thought.

"I'm heading back," he said, "We had to get away for awhile. I had got a job in Alberta, worked in a goldmine for a couple a years, hated it, but put together a little cash and decided it's time to come home. We're in Ohio. Should be there tomorrow. The place OK? Elijah?"

Ella shook her head at the phone, acknowledged she heard what Sam told her, and hung up. "Elijah won't be waiting for you," she said to the now silent receiver. The phone rang again and she thought, we'll talk about this in due time, Sam.

Ella stepped outside and off the porch as two sheriff cars and an ambulance stopped along the road and two men and two women in uniforms hastened along the driveway, the deputies with guns drawn. Carter put her pistol back inside her parker. This is going to take a little time, she thought, with cartons of meals yet to deliver.

Ella ignored the new visitors and their uniforms, walked over to Malcolm, and put a hand on his shoulder. She liked him more than she had admitted.

"Sam and Margaret are coming back. They'll want their place" she said. "You can handle that?"

What? he thought. He looked at her blankly and tried to process what he just heard.

"We'll see," he said after a pause. Another defining moment.

As the two EMTs relieved Jessup and tended to Edwards, one of the deputies, a woman, nametag said Shirley McCord, walked over to Marie, who explained what happened. She pointed in the direction Elijah had taken.

Ella moved her hand down Malcolm's arm.

"Go with them and take the dogs," she said. "They'll find him. When you come back, we'll talk."

Live in the attic? I don't think so.

Malcolm remembered himself thinking that when he left the sisters after giving his statement to police. The police might single him out and call him in for further questioning, probably hassle him a little. Enough of that. He was free. Time to move on.

When he said his goodbyes, the sisters told him Elijah was in the guarded fifth floor of McKinley Hospital, most often heavily sedated. Edwards ended up in that hospital too but since was released. He had decided he had enough of rural New York and returned to his apartment in Harrisburg, Pennsylvania. Time to look for another way to do things.

"Me too," Malcolm said to himself.

Sam was back, he could help the sisters now. Malcolm knew he'd miss them, though, especially Ella.

The truck bed camper was back on the pickup, the vehicle rocking from side-to-side as he rode down the lowest segment of Claw Valley Pike, the broken asphalt part. It started to snow. He thought about Corey.

THE FOG

The fog. Enoch felt secure in its midst.

It muted city sounds. It was a cloak that left him with the sensation that he was connected with a visible spirit, yet separate, suspended.

Sitting on a bench near a subway station in lower Manhattan, he thought back to a decisive day in his young life, another morning in the fog when he walked down a Queens street to a candy story. Very similar, he thought. Then he was 12. Now, he's 17.

He had always seemed to himself out of place. True, he played with others then, stickball in the schoolyard, punchball, stoopball, roller hockey on the streets, was good at it. But there was a division between all this and him that he wasn't able to fathom.

"Maybe it's my name," he remembered himself thinking while walking in the fog that day down narrow 208th Street in Queens to the store -- "Enoch Jubal." Some his age called him "Jewboy".

Actually, he could have argued that his Hungarian-born grandfather was a Catholic, his grandmother a Lutheran, and he was confirmed in the Catholic church. His grandfather had an Austrian name, Rothpauer, but his drinking buddies called him "Rummy." "Rummy Jewboy," the young boys said, teasing, when Enoch let on about his grandfather's nickname.

These two days in the fog meshed. He barely noticed people's haste as they exited and entered the subway stairway near him. Back then, he recalled, a wisp of mist had risen from a manhole cover toward him as he walked, with a sewer scent. He remembered letting himself feel enveloped by it. Now, it was the musty odor from the underground, from up the subway. It too enveloped him.

"No, it was just me," he thought.

Musing, he recollected hearing a boy's voice call to him in the fog as he neared a corner on his walk.

"Enoch! Hey, up here," the boy called.

It was Barry, a Jewish friend he sometimes hung out with, though Barry's mother didn't approve. Barry had climbed a maple tree.

"Where ya goin'?"

"Down to Dinks."

"Yeah, okay. I can't go, my mother wants me to stay around. Get me a candy bar, will ya, a Baby Ruth."

"You got any money?"

"A quarter." Barry tossed it onto the sidewalk.

"Okay. I'm keeping the change. Don't fall." Enoch said.

This was just a year after the end of World War II, which he had followed in the newspapers from third grade on, remembering Franklin D. Roosevelt's Day of Infamy speech on the radio, after Japanese planes bombed Pearl Harbor. He had also followed the first atomic bomb tests at Alamogordo, New Mexico and Bikini Atoll, reading about the concern that a nuclear chain reaction from the explosions could uncontrollably erupt throughout the world. Then there were the A-bomb devastations of Hiroshima and Nagasaki.

He remembered experiencing too the brown B-47 bombers flying low overhead in Queens en route to the war, the air-raid drills and the blackouts, V-E day when the Allies finally defeated Hitler's armies and neighborhood people ran out into the night to celebrate with shouts, banging pots and pans, and V-J Day as well, when Japan surrendered, and the neighbors celebrated again.

Except those who had the little flag in a window of their house or apartment that indicated someone in their family was killed in battle. It was always a curiosity on the street to see a new flag up.

"Look, Enoch," a neighborhood boy, Kirk, had said when the war was nearing its end, as they walked along 33rd Avenue. "There's another one."

"Isn't that where one of the teachers lives?," Enoch remembered asking. "Mrs. O'Brien?"

"Yeah, and her son. Denny," Kirk answered. "He always acted like he was a big shot."

It was, also, he knew in his newspaper reading, a time of anticipation of the Korean conflict that again would take thousands of military lives. He'd be too young for that one when it came. Just by a hair. Now it was over.

Though beginning to fail in school back then, he read the newspapers and kept up on the war news, thinking that military conflicts didn't make sense to him. Especially the casualties, the atrocities, the holocaust. He read sports news as well, the heroics, the statistics, about the players, and collected baseball cards that would mysteriously disappear at home, mostly likely thrown out.

Homework was out of the question for him in the rented three-room flat he had shared with his mother, brother and grandparents, upstairs in a two-family house, especially the times when his grandfather came home drunk and he'd be manhandled, once even picked up and thrown against a wall, or shoved repeatedly against a refrigerator. It was supposed to toughen him up. Occasionally, he'd be sent on bicycle to a corner tavern in Bayside West to tell his grandfather it was time to come home, which he both dreaded and looked forward to as a challenge. On the bench, Enoch smiled at how that encounter would go..

"Pops, Grandma wants you. Better get in your car and come home," he'd say.

"Look who's got the balls to tell me what to do," his grandfather would reply. Something like that. "Get your ass out of here. You're as stupid as your father." Then his grandfather would laugh, more like a cackle, turn his back, and drink his shot and a beer.

Times with his grandfather became worse after the war when his job ended at the Farmingdale, Long Island plant that built P-47 Thunderbolt fighter planes. It would be a couple of humiliating years before he'd find work again, ending up as a machinist in a paper goods factory in Queens. His grandmother was drinking heavily too, usually loopy by suppertime.

An evening ritual for Enoch was to feel the radiator of his grandfather's faded black Dodge parked on the street. If it was warm, he'd still be up. Not a good time to go in. His younger brother Jimmy was occasionally hovering nearby.

"Still warm," Jimmy said one time, he remembered. "Where you been?"

"Around. In the park for awhile. Mom's not home?"

"No. Late bus hasn't come yet."

Enoch's mother Anne was the mainstay support during that difficult period with her job as a film hand at Paramount's studios in Manhattan. His father, Seth, lived alone in Manhattan in a small midtown hotel on 9th Avenue, a brooding free-lance illustrator who had been blacklisted because of union organizing at a magazine. With him, there was little contact and no financial support. And Enoch usually only saw his younger brother at home. There was little exchange between them beyond that.

In the fog then and now, Enoch wondered why he felt so confusingly separate. He thought about how he hated to fight when challenged by other boys. When he wouldn't, they'd hoot and call him "chicken shit!" He wouldn't steal candy bars at Dinks either as challenged, though he began to linger, not just to look at comics but also women's shapes in magazines, feeling a growing sensation in his body.

"You gonna buy one of those?" Jim Dinks asked on his walk then. "No, just the paper," he replied. It was usually the Daily Mirror, with photos, though sometimes he bought the Herald Tribune and slipped a magazine inside when Dinks was preoccupied with other customers. He'd hide the magazine in the back of a billboard he sometimes crawled behind if there wasn't somebody homeless there.

Enoch remembered first feeling that sensation in the neighborhood park, when he was shinnying down the angled bars that held the swings upright. "Don't you ever do that again," his mother berated when he mentioned it to her. He was stung. Then he realized. Nobody told him.

He thought, "Hell, you should talk," realizing even more, she propped up at night reading mysteries in a thin nightgown in her chair bed while he and his brother went to sleep on a fold-down couch in the same room. He had discovered her notes about a married man named Bob from a diary she thought she kept hidden.

He remembered becoming more acutely aware, too, of two girl neighbors along his street, of Noreen's laughing eyes and Dolores's coy smile, and their sinewyness. He had daydreamed how he would rescue them from an onrushing car and they'd love him, explore him and he'd be connected. Dolores was the first to wear lipstick and began to flirt around. Noreen was athletic, the first one he deeply kissed and held, merged together in the dark alley between two houses, she in her sister's hand-me-down dress. Noreen also shared a cramped second floor apartment in a two-family house with her sister and mother. In their living room window was one of the flags that indicated a war death, in memory of her father. Enoch only knew Noreen's sister and mother to say hello.

Then there were his escapes, like when he'd have enough small change to dare sneak off for a bus and subway excursion throughout the city. He knew the routes. Or his frequent solitary bike rides to Crocheron Park, over a wooden bridge above the Cross Island Parkway to Little Neck Bay, locking the bike, walking along the sand's edge, the water polluted, yet gentle against the shore. He loved that edge. Days in school were meaningless, disconnected, abstract. Home was a wrench on his head. The streets were different. Then, as now, they were his refuge, his education.

"I should run away," he thought over and over then. It wouldn't take much. He didn't fear running away; he feared being caught and brought back again.

That day, a little more than four years ago, coming out of Dinks, the fog drifted, broke up and dissipated. If he could only disappear with it, he had thought.

"Now I'm gone," he said to himself on the bench. He had formally quit school a year ago, obtained working papers, and gotten a job cleaning out a meat lockers near the Hudson River waterfront. He obtained as well a room in a small hotel in lower Manhattan near Houston Street, a walkup rooming house really, with a bathroom at the end the hall. It was noisy but he didn't mind. The owner and others there were friendly and the room was furnished. Better than the streets and the abandoned buildings he lived in, evading searches for his whereabouts, one among hundreds of city street kids, working in the underground economy, the fish and produce markets, hawking newspapers for distributors, odd jobs. sometimes begging. He had seen and eluded his father and grandfather looking for him, both who knew the streets too. Enoch felt seasoned, savvy.

Occasionally now, somewhat settled, he'd have lunch with his mother at a midtown automat restaurant, who pouted when she chided him about running away. He'd hook up with his brother, too, who was still in school but who would take the bus and train to Manhattan. The two still lived with his grandparents and tried to persuade him to return. He declined. He couldn't imagine how they tolerated it. Sometimes he'd join his father for breakfast at a corner midtown luncheonette, Seth ever brooding, but eking out a living. Enoch had passed on staying with him as well, now in another cramped hotel room he moved into on Eighth Avenue.

Enough, he thought. Enoch rose from the bench

and walked toward the Hudson River, a few blocks away. The fog was lifting. It was time for another decision. Noreen phoned the rooming house to tell him she was on her way to meet him. She'd be at Washington Square Park.

Many times since running away he had snuck into his old neighborhood to connect with her. Something between them persisted, more than the encounters that had grown more passionate each time they met. She was smart, had graduated from high school early, was ready to strike out, get a full-time job, maybe even look into going to City College of New York. Enoch couldn't figure out what she saw in him, but it didn't matter.

He reached a wharf at the river's edge, kneeled on the planks, and looked into the water as it slapped against the pilings. Noreen said she was bringing a suitcase. A suitcase, he thought. He stood up, looked at the river, turned, grinned, and walked toward the park.

SCOOTER

Below, in the hollow, Madelaine Krutcher adjusted herself on the floor where she fell trying to retrieve a bottle of gin from the kitchen inside her 40-year-old house, nested among tall loblolly pines, tulip trees, sweet gums and maples. She launched into a harangue as she tried to sit up.

"Hate this thing, what, quad cane, fell again, but no one's falling for me, don't they know I'm a Red Hat girl, damn legs swollen," she said as if someone was there. "Cat tripped me, Snookie sweet pup lick my face, Nippy, you're ignoring me - Now they want me to have a motorized wheel chair, little ramps on my hardwood floor."

She had fallen in a hallway alongside three uncleaned litter boxes. Her elbow was in one, part of her robe in another. She was barefoot.

"Feel me, feel my skin, feel it all - nobody touches me - I'm the nice one with cute little dogs, lots of cats. Doctor says at my age, what, I need a health care worker. If he's a man OK, otherwise, skip it."

Krutcher removed her arm from the cat litter with what she thought was a gesture of grace, pretending she was on stage.

"Drink, drink, drink, I need a drink, a man too, Horace is gone, other one also, husband, what was his name? Age makes you forget but how could I forget that. Rusty, Rusty was lusty, dead too. Oh can't get up. Oh no, not Rusty . . . Russell! -- Damn I gotta get up, nobody's going to help me."

Her monologues like this became frequent, nasty in tone. She liked to hear her voice, thought she should have been an actress, a femme fatal. Never too late, she believed.

"Y'all see me out there," she said to the living room uttering a laugh. "I'm a gonna get up. I expect applause."

She managed to rise, stabilize herself uneasily on her cane, and reach for the bottle of gin on the black formica countertop in the kitchen. She returned to the screened-in back porch where earlier she had carried a melting tray of ice, a tall floral glass and a bottle of tonic, now on an opaque glass patio table. She sat unsteadily in a lawn chair, filled the glass, took a long drink and shouted;

"You out there, you damn coyote? You the one who was jumping at the porch door for my little pup Nippy?"

A canine chorus of dogs had begun their nightsong of barking from other homes in the older subdivision carved into the steeply bounded hollow.

"Oh yes, oh yes, sing it, sing it. You hear that Nippy, they're singing to you and me?" Nippy made a little motion with his tail but otherwise didn't move. Snookie was off somewhere.

"Snookie," she called. "Snookie, get out here and keep me company. Coyote, you out there?"

Above, on the ridge overlooking Krutcher's home, stood Billy Skype, short, disheveled, in his 30s, eyes focusing and unfocusing in the fading late summer twilight, sweating in the heat in front of a double-wide mobile home where a couple inside were cooking enough meth for tonight and tomorrow, they said.

He, too, was ranting, but softly, with little rhythm, shifting his shoulders, his neck, imagining himself rapping, more like mouthing the words. He sat on a rock, unsteady, near the only vehicle he could ride now.

"Floating, sweet. Don't need a license for the scooter in this state, feels like riding on rubber, frame liquid, flowing, rocking, rolling, what speed, so so high, shimmer shimmer, shudder, up to Cliff's and Samantha's, cooking it, smoking it, out again."

He thought he was good enough to be recorded even though shouts of "shut the fuck up" yowled when he let loose in the county jail he just left.

"Book me, fuckers, I'm out of there, nobody I am, nobody but the scooter under my legs, swirling, surfing. There's that little lady again down in the holler where Cliff shot golf balls, to somewhere down there, laughing, using a golf club, where the hell did he get them all from, he called them goof balls, funny man." Oh yeah, this is good, Billy mused to himself.

"Little lady on the back porch, with a bottle, must be vodka, got to pay her a visit. Place might be nice, this one's a mess, electricity water all turned off, candles, propane, love the flickering, what they doing now those two inside?" He wanted to join in but knew they weren't into that.

"Little lady want a visitor? I'm the one the SWAT team snared when I threatened to kill myself after I scared off my lady friend in that house by the state park, shit, one year is all they took from me, then rehab, what fools, what a joke. Little lady, I'm a rapper with a rap sheet, I'm bad, you want bad?"

So Skype and Krutcher met one day in a supermarket parking lot. It really wasn't an accident. This was before the fire. He had noticed her drive off and followed as well as he could. He helped her carry her package from the liquor store into her van. She thanked him.

Shelly and Corey Rose, neighbors, generally shopped on Wednesdays for groceries when senior-citizens discounts were granted. Shelly would retrieve Krutcher's shopping list as well. On the way back, they'd pull into Krutcher's drive two houses up the hill from theirs, and though Corey helped unload Krutcher's groceries, he usually declined to go inside, leaving the packages on Krutcher's small front porch for Shelly to bring inside.

"The way she comes on, it makes me uncomfortable," Corey said.

"I know," Shelly said. "Madelaine worries me, she's a stubborn lady. I'm always struck by her bright-eyes look, like it covers a darkness. What a mess, her place."

Corey opened the car's side door and picked up a bag containing four jars of scented candles and held them up. He grinned.

Shelly shrugged.

"Corey. You come in this one time too. She wants to know about the revolver in her kitchen drawer. You know that."

Shelly would visit Krutcher weekly, sometimes clean the cat litter, concerned about what she felt was

Krutcher's increasing immobility and immodesty, drinking, and lack of self-care.

"She falls, she drinks, her legs have swelled, she shouldn't be driving, and she looks jaundiced sometimes," she told Corey. "She might be having liver problems. She's hinted at that. It doesn't look good. Now, there's the revolver."

Like other neighbors who occasionaly visited, Shelly had suggested Krutcher make arrangements for a health care worker, and like others, she had been rebuffed. Once in awhile Krutcher would walk into her front yard and street with a cane in her red bathrobe, one dog on a leash, the other loose. If neighbors were out, she'd visit with them, seeming composed and measured. Otherwise, she'd let her dogs out into her fenced-in backyard that abutted the woodlands in back.

"You coming in?" Shelly asked Corey.

Corey carried the scented candles and two other bags into Krutcher's house, skirted the animals, the bright-eyes, the poses, the unsettlng tone, the elegant furniture pieces that needed cleaning, and noted the odor. "Cats. I should light one of the candles," he said to himself.

He opened a kitchen drawer Krutcher pointed to and pulled out a small .32-caliber revolver. It was loaded. Krutcher moved to his side. Corey removed the bullets and suggested it remain unloaded.

"You know how to shoot?" he asked.

"No, I should learn? It was Russell's. I'm a widow, you know," she answered, touching his arm. "I should know how? For protection?"

Krutcher smiled.

Corey replaced the pistol in the drawer, the bullets toward the back.

"It's too dangerous," he said.

It was the next Saturday morning in the hollow, early, and Corey was in the kitchen making coffee when he heard a loud pop outside. He stepped into the back yard, glanced into the woods behind his house and heard a man shout for help from up the ridge.

Corey looked through woodland foliage. Flames began to swell upward behind trees and burning timber crackled. The odor of smoke hadn't reached him yet but the fire appeared well underway in the direction of a double-wide on the ridge's edge.

The man called again as he descended the steep incline from the ridge. "The house. It's on fire! Help me!"

Corey's first reaction was to wonder whether the fire would spread downward and if he should warn neighbors. He rushed back into the kitchen for his cell phone and called 9-1-1, woke Shelly, then walked quickly through his next door neighbor's backyard toward Krutcher's house, closer to the fire. The fire wasn't descending, but the double-wide he saw through the trees was definitely engulfed. Looking past Krutcher's house, he saw her neighbor on the other side standing in his backyard, talking into a phone. With him was another man, eyes staring, seated on a stump, no doubt the one who called for help. Corey heard sirens close in on the ridge and in a short time could hear water rushing from hoses and firefighters shouting.

"He's in shock," the neighbor, Mark Rivers, said, turning his head toward the seated man. "He said his girlfriend ran back into the house to get her dog. She didn't come out."

The meth house, it must be the meth house, Corey thought, looking at the man who called for help. Other neighbors were now outside in the hollow, on the street below the fire, nodding. Yes, it's the meth house, was the refrain. Police have been there before, the place was without power and water. Was it candles? Meth cooking that started the fire? As the firefighters doused the blaze, one neighbor said she once saw the woman from the double-wide casing a house from her car on an adjoining street.

"Just parked there," she said. "Broad daylight."

Shelly joined Corey, now in front of Krutcher's house.

"Madelaine awake?," she asked.

"Who knows?" Corey answered. "It doesn't seem so."

He turned his head in the direction of an small dirty scooter that was parked close to the side of Krutcher's garage under a tree.

"I wonder where that came from?"

They had never seen it before.

Corey and Shelly were retired educators yet active both with computer and internet technology and, over the decades, in social-justice causes. They decided to check the county's GIS tax map to see what they could learn about the double-wide. Their search revealed that the property was listed in Samantha Stillwell's name, the person who news reports said died in the fire. Further searching, they found a news item about Jenny Stillwell of the same address who had once been charged with manufacturing methamphetamine. She had been booked with a man named Billy Skype.

Police photos of both were online. They downloaded the photos.

News reports also mentioned Cliff Dodd as the survivor of the fire, that he had no address listing, and that he had been questioned and released. He was presumed to be homeless. County sheriff booking reports contained nothing about him and there were no photos. The news reports also mentioned that the fire was under investigation, that electrical, natural gas and water utilities were shut off for nonpayment, and that much of the dwelling had been destroyed. There was no mention of a dog.There were no obituaries listed for Samantha Stillwell either.

"We'll go up and look at this," Corey said.

"Let's do it when things quiet down a little," Shelly responded.

Two days later, on a curving ridge road, they saw the destruction, the remains of a police line tape, melted vinyl siding on the ground, and most of the double-wide charred, its insides exposed, the odor of smoke still present. Walking around the lot, they saw a number of old golf balls on the driveway's edge.

"Looks like a driving range," Corey said. "I wonder if somebody worked in one here?

A man with cropped white hair in a white T-shirt and jeans walked toward them from farther up the road.

"Can I help y'all? he called.

He identified himself as Skip Walker, owner of the adjacent property, about 10 acres into the woodlands, he said. Shelly and Corey identified themselves.

"You know these folks? You got business here?" Walker asked.

"No," Corey said. "We're being curious. You can see our place down below, through the trees. I was one of those who called 9-1-1."

"These folks and what went on there make me very cautious," Walker said. "I didn't want them heading up to my place. They were a damned nuisance. And I'm also suspicious about people picking around this mess."

"Did you get to know them at all?," Shelly asked.

Walker shook his head no.

"I challenged what they were up to but they laughed, told me to 'F' off. Police were here a few times. I never called, but others on the ridge did. I have no idea how they managed with no power or water."

A thought came to Corey: "You ever see a scooter up here? I noticed one parked by Madelaine Krutcher's house, down there."

"Really," Walker said. He looked over the ridge.

"Yes, a little one, old, beat up, just recently," he answered. "I know who Madelaine is. She always seemed like a nice lady. Husband died awhile back. She seemed to keep to herself mostly. No relatives as far as I know except a nephew in Georgia somewhere. We didn't have much contact."

"We help her out with groceries, look after her a little," Shelly said.

Walker nodded. "What the hell would the scooter be doing down there?," he mused.

"Looks like we got ourselves a little complication," Corey said.

"Seems so."

"I'm going to check on Madelaine," Shelly said as they drove back into the hollow. "Drop me off." Corey pulled into Krutcher's driveway. The scooter was still parked alongside the garage.

"I'll wait here," he said. "Just in case."

Shelly walked up porch stairs to the front door and knocked. No answer. She tried the door, it was open. She signaled to Corey that she was going inside. Walking quietly through the gloom of the living room she saw a shirtless man sprawled across the couch, sleeping under a comforter. The room smelled of cigarette smoke and alcohol. She tiptoed past him to a bedroom and there Madelaine lay sleeping as well, diagonally on her bad, covered by her robe. Shelly could see into the kitchen and on the table was the revolver, two wine bottles, a prescription vial, and a bra. She turned, the man stirred, but appeared to remain asleep. Shelly opened the front door quietly and left.

"You wouldn't believe it," she said to Corey as she entered their vehicle. "Her bra and the pistol were on the kitchen table. Remember the guy in the photos we downloaded? He was on the couch, Madeleine was in the bedroom. I don't think they had clothes on under what covered them."

"What is this guy about with her?" Corey asked. "I think we got to look into this even more deeply, know more about him."

"She's within her rights, we have to be sensitive" Shelly said. "I'll call Pat across the street, see what she knows." Corey replied that he'd check also with Tom Olden, their neighbor whose house abutted Krutcher's.

From the calls, they determined that their neighbors were on alert as well, that Pat Ainsworth had tried to look in on Krutcher but was met at the door by a man who didn't identify himself but who said he was looking after Madelaine now, that Madelaine wanted him to do that, and that Pat should mind her own business. Tom Olden and his wife Sally and daughter Terry were also keeping an eye out, had seen the man driving Madelaine's van once and returning with the plastic bag used by the Red Branch Spirits liquor store, plus some groceries.

Corey printed out the photo of Billy Skype along with news items of his arrests and bookings and gave them to the neighbors. The shared notion was that Krutcher was being preyed on.

When Shelly came to the front door, Billy Skype had heard the knock, then the door open. He listened and stayed still. Someone's inside, he thought. He could see it was a woman. and pretended to be asleep. "What is this about," he whispered to himself.

He waited until she left, then got up from the couch, wrapped himself in the comforter, composed himself, and looked through the window blinds in time to see Corey and Shelly pull out of the driveway, motor down the hill, and enter a driveway two houses down.

"Fuckers," he said.

He felt like his head was in a wrench and reached for the prescription vial on the kitchen table -- oxycodone, it belonged to Madeleine. He removed two pills, put them in his mouth, brought one of the wine bottles to his mouth, and drank. He picked up the revolver, checked the chamber, it was still loaded.

"The bitch didn't remove the bullets," he said. He pointed the barrel at the broad living room mirror, saw himself and laughed, loud.

"I'm bad, I'm sad, I oughta kill that dude in the mirror," he said. "What's he up to now, messing with an old lady, bad, sad, pathetic dude." He felt dizzy and reached for the kitchen drawer. He put the revolver inside.

"Not today," he said.

"Damn right, not today, especially not here," said a voice from the bedroom. "Get me my cane."

"You ain't ordering me around," Skype said.

"You don't want me to call police and report you as an intruder. Get me my damn cane," Krutcher said. "And pour me a glass of wine."

Skype complied and mentioned that he saw a woman come in and look around, one from down the street.

"I know," Krutcher said. "It was Shelly. Got a cute husband, my age. Not a fool like you. She was checking if I was okay?"

"You know about me a little," Skype said. "What do you think?"

"It doesn't matter," Krutcher answered. "This is probably my last go-round. You could be a coyote for all they know, in spite of what you told me. Coyotes prey on the weak. The question is, who's the real coyote?" Krutcher laughed and had a coughing fit.

Skype's eyes scanned the kitchen. He wondered again whether she kept a stash of money in the house. She read this.

"I don't keep any money around here, except what I need. You know that. I gave you some to buy the groceries. You know where that is. That's it until I get to the bank again. If I get there."

Krutcher sat down at the kitchen table, sipped her wine to ease her coughing, looked at her pain pills, opened the vial and swallowed one, then handed the vial to Skype. The physical weakness she would frequently feel returned. She felt like sagging.

"I know you like these," she said. She placed her hand on his arm. "I know you're in pain. This'll help. But I'm telling you also I'm done here with you. You can be on your way, you and your scooter and your coyote ass. When you go, you better get yourself checked. I've got septicemia, blood poisoning. They want me to fight it, but I got no fight left."

Krutcher looked at Skype clinically. Though she had mostly been a housewife, widowed twice, she knew she was smart. She also felt worn. She was on to him a little, she thought. Something beat him down and he's not going to be able to get up. She watched him remove a few pills from the vial and swallow them. He emptied one of the bottles of wine.

"You know I do know you had some connection with those people in the meth house that caught fire," she said. "What that means to you, if anything, is your business. Me, I'm going to get drunk."

They both drank the second bottle of wine, turned inward for awhile, and began their private rants, thinking of the other as an audience, not really listening at first. Then, as if it were improv theater, they played their voices off each other, a vocal dance, she getting up and hobbling around waving one arm in what she felt were graceful sweeps, he stomping, hitting his head with his hands, pumping his arms to the ceiling, both laughing and crying, vocalizing, words clashing, hanging in the room, spiraling, connecting and then returning to the one who shouted, sang and mourned them. The fatigue left Krutcher, but Skype stopped, appeared to try to catch his breath, held his chest, and fell on the hardwood floor.

Femme fatale, Krutcher thought. "I better call 9-1-1."

Corey heard sirens close to his house and stepped outside. An ambulance stopped in front of Madelaine Krutcher's house.

"What now," he said to himself. He joined other neighbors who stood together along Krutcher's driveway. Two emergency medical technicians entered the home through the front door, came back out, retrieved a stretcher, and re-entered. He noticed the scooter was parked where he first saw it.

Krutcher opened the door, wearing her red robe, walked out onto the porch and raised both arms.

"Not me," she said. "My friend passed out. He held his chest and fell to the floor."

She smiled, her eyes aglow, and moved aside as the EMTs came back out with the stretcher. It was empty. They returned it to the ambulance, one sat behind the steering wheel in the cab and talked on the vehicle's radio, the other stood near its open back doors.

"Absurd," a neighbor remarked. Others chuckled as they waited to see what might happen next. The front door opened a few moments later and Billy Skype appeared. He wore a white tee-shirt and jeans, eased himself slowly down the porch stairs, and stepped awkwardly onto the driveway as if he was unsure of his footing. He was smoking a cigarette.

"Stoned," someone whispered. "Good lord," another said in a low voice.

Skype slowly walked toward the ambulance, scowling at his audience, stopped in front of the technician and continued to smoke his cigarette.

Trouble with his balance, Corey thought. And a little show of defiance to go along with all this.

Skype dropped the cigarette, still lit, turned to the EMT, was helped inside the ambulance, and they left. Krutcher returned inside her home without another word. The neighbors looked at each other, some chatted.

"It gets odder, doesn't it," Corey said, smiling, as he headed back home. There were nods in agreement.

That night, a taxicab returned Skype to Krutcher's house. The next day the scooter was gone. Three days later, an ambulance was in Krutcher's driveway. This time it came for her.

Shelly, with a key from Krutcher, had been feeding Krutcher's pets in her absence. Corey hid the pistol separate from the bullets, and he, Shelly and other neighbors kept watch for Skype. Not long after, a tan Lincoln with Georgia plates pulled into Krutcher's driveway. Shelly spoke with the driver who identified himself as Krutcher' nephew, Sam Oliver. He said he was her only living relative and had power of attorney, granted by Krutcher when she knew her illness was getting worse.

"It doesn't look good," Oliver said. "She's on a ventilator."

In the follwing days, neighbors said thought they saw Skype as a passenger in a pickup truck that slowly passed the house. Skype was also reported to have tried to visit Krutcher at the hospital but was denied entrance into the intensive care ward where she remained unconscious, on life support.

Corey and Shelly decided to bring one of Krutcher's cats into their home as the other cats and two dogs were brought to a veterinarian. When Corey checked, a technician told him they'd find a home for the pets if Krutcher died.

"She's a lovely lady," the technician said.

"So they say," Corey said.

That night Krutcher died.

Three days later police made inquiries about Skype, asking the Roses' nextdoor neighbors whether they believed he had anything to do with Krutcher's death. They told the police it was unlikely, she was very ill when he came around. That was the last people in the hollow heard from the police about Krutcher's death or from Skype.

Billy Skype had tried to find Cliff Dodd after the meth house fire with no success. After Krutcher's death he made another attempt, visiting the city's homeless center, where he'd have his meals, as well as other shelters. No luck. Dodd wasn't seen in jail either. His whereabouts were unknown. Skype sought to find out if police or fire investigators were pursuing a probe of the double-wide's fire. They apparently weren't.

Skype also checked the daily newspaper at the city library for word about Krutcher and eventually found her obituary. She was buried in the cemetery on Memorial Boulevard, near a pond where ducks lived year around. He rode there in his scooter, parked it, searched for her marker, found it, and sat on the ground next to it. He opened a plastic bag, pulled out a bottle of red wine and two transparent plastic cups and poured wine into each. He placed one next to the marker, raised his, sipped from it until it was empty, then placed her cup inside his.

"Little lady, I'm bad. You want bad?"

He placed the wine battle next to the two cups, kneeling.

"The rest is for you," he said.

TINA'S NICARAGUA STORY

(Nonfiction)

We met Florentina Pérez Calderón in 1992, when my spouse Eileen and I had traveled to Nicaragua to engage in human rights exploration. With two U.S. friends who lived there, we traveled to the northern area that bordered Honduras, a border transgressed repeatedly during the 1980s by invading "Contras." The U.S. supported the Contras, who were armed to violently interfere with the Sandinista socialist government that was partly administered by two Nicaraguan Catholic priests who backed popular movements. Two years before our arrival, the Contra invasion climaxed in a U.S. brokered election that brought into power a government amenable to U.S. interests.

Florentina's daughter Maria Zunilda and husband José Angel had been killed in a Contra onslaught. She shared leadership in one of the small cooperatives in the north that made up El Bloqué (the Bloc), and greeted us when we arrived in her base community near the village of Achuapa. El Bloqué was a popular movement developed to help those in the north survive.

Tina, as she was called, related her story as we walked one morning along a trail toward a river gorge mostly parched in the midst of a drought. Her people, generations ago, had been driven off their land near León to the south by cotton and banana plantation interests and so were forced to eke out a living in the less fertile and often inhospitable hills to the north. Earlier that morning, Tina had ground sorghum, sugar cane stalks, in a hand grinder and on a hand-stone mill for tortillas, using sorghum because all their corn was depleted. Visitors and friends who worked with the Bloqué helped her, including Jenny Atlee-Loudon, and her husband Tom, formerly with Witness for Peace, in Nicaragua with their then 3-year-old daughter Carmen. They had quarters in nearby Achuapa, living out what they considered to be an option of solidarity with the oppressed and helping to supplement scant resources through North American connections.

Tina had been making the stack of tortillas for community children who would be heading into the village for the next week, where the children shared a room so they could go to school in a newer building village men were fixing up. The old schoolhouse was where her husband was killed in the Contra attack, the building burned down. There was a shrine to him in Tina's small brick hut. Another shrine was for her daughter, who confronted this same Contra onslaught on the base community.

Her daughter, Maria Zunilda, on the day of the attack, according to the story, had brought the community's extremely thin cows to a hillock to feed on the parched land there. She carried with her a carbine rifle, customary because of the ongoing threat of Contra attacks. On the hill, she heard the community's sentry yell "The Contras are invading." They overran and killed him. Maria Zunilda could see from her vantage that her community companions wouldn't have time enough to completely flee the attack. Tina knew her daughter was on the hill and shouted a warning to her not to engage the Contras.

"I'm going to fight," she reportedly shouted back.

Maria Zunilda rushed down the hill and positioned herself between the fleeing community members and the oncoming Contras and began to fire her rifle at the invaders. Her action delayed the onslaught just enough to enable her community companions to escape safely. She was overrun too.

Both Tina's daughter and husband were killed in late 1984 -- a little more than seven years had passed when we were there. The community had still survived, obstinate but fragile. "The martyrs, they keep the communities together," another woman said a few days later, in another base community near the northern border town of Somotillo, also part of the Bloqué. "The martyrs' spirits are real, alive" she said, "They sometimes reappear to give words of encouragement, to bring light. They are ancestors of hope."

Along the trail Tina guided us, toward the river to the left, she gestured to a cascade of rocks. Fleeing members had rushed headlong over these rocks to escape the Contras during the attack, she said, taking the most difficult route to elude their pursuers. Another base community nearby, just further down to the left, maybe a mile, had been totally wiped out. One of its male organizers was dropped alive, she said, from a helicopter onto a pile of bodies below. Contras decapitated a woman leader in the same attack, her head rolled around like a soccer ball. "Just over there," Tina said, "past that ridge of trees." Tina walked her history, a via dolorosa; invigorated it with a fierceness, a burden and a cross that fired a refusal to capitulate, I thought.

As Tina and others noted, the martyrs bore fierce power. Their shrines combined the images and memories of the community's dead with Christian images of the Christ of the poor, in their minds, and with emblems of popular movement practice. They also appeared, in this view, to open a kind of spiritual-material liberationist space. More than saints of the Christian past, they were tangible. controversial, not canonized, members of families, who became beloved ancestors, heroes of particular sites of resistance. The communities' apparitions were connected to an indigenous spirituality, a Nicaraguan mestizo form which expressed itself partly through Christian practice but also had its own authenticity.

Tina said she herself had seen and been inspired by such visitations from her own kin. She reflected practically on all this during our walk.

"Base-community members are people," she said, "with all the weaknesses and strengths people have. Some go on binges. Others slack off when work needs to be done. Still others are continually difficult to live with."

With two loved ones killed, and with hopeful children needing a future, she vowed she would persist. For her, the practical and material side of divinity was where the work goes on.

One little coda --   Juan Pérez, a young community man disabled by polio, who couldn't walk, thus couldn't flee the Contra onslaught, escaped by dragging himself by his arms into the community latrine. From there he became Maria Zunilda's eyewitness.

Openng the Gate   --   Wes Rehberg

JAIL BIRDS

The guard brought me to a tiny room with a small wooden table and two chairs. He opened the door, showed me the button to push if I needed help and told me to take a chair. The guard then walked toward the county jail's cells to retrieve an itinerant young man, accused of murdering a boy, 14-years-old. The charges alleged that the accused man killed the boy, strangled him, after he keyed a scratch on the man's car door. I was there because he requested a jail minister. This was during a time I volunteered to do prison ministry. Now, years later, I find myself musing about his situation and others I encountered in this work. Especially those that involved homicides. I'm also writing this as a way of thinking back on things. It seems appropriate now.

I looked over a review of his case that day and saw that it included these items:

He was a young itinerant man who was closely involved with the boy: this was one allegation. He set himself up in an upstate New York truck stop as a "chrome polisher," one who reputedly not only looked for odd jobs shining chrome on trucks, but also performed sexual favors for money: another item imputed to him. He had a reputation for volatile outbursts: a third.

A fourth allegation said that the young man reportedly let the boy sleep in his car, where he slept too. A fifth indicated that the accused just bought the car, a used vehicle, shined it up, had apparently felt the pride of possession and was outraged at the scratch the boy was supposed to have etched into the paint. There may have been more. For me, this was enough to know.

As I often did then, I wondered what compelled this prisoner to want to see a minister, what my role could be. I also wondered how I felt about being locked in a tiny interview room with this one. It puzzled me, too, how the boy that the accused was alleged to have killed could have been so free to continue to encounter him in the way described. Media coverage suggested a few answers: the 14-year-old was basically a street kid, a frequent truant who lived with an ailing grandfather. The two were both clients of overworked Social Service employees whose case loads had grown too large for them to handle. Neither the boy nor his grandfather had a record of involvement in criminal activity. The boy's mother died from a heroin overdose about six months previous and had been arrested several times for prostitution.

More deeply for me, jail visits such as this one had prompted another, maybe more direct, question. Was I in the right profession as a minister? I had strong doubts.

The guard returned to the room with a man who was slim, of medium height, disheveled, with brown hair and blue eyes, and guided the man to a chair. He locked the door. The man stood across from me in the confining space, wild-eyed. He smelled like sweat. I asked him his name. I knew it, of course. The question was an ice-breaker.

"God hates me," the man said loudly, looking at me. "God hates me for what I did."

"What's your name," I asked again, quietly.

"Do you hear me?" he asked. "You're a minister, God hates me? Why?"

"Please tell me your name."

He paused, leaned back, brushed his hair to one side with his hand. "Jimmy Neal," he answered.

"Have a seat, Jimmy. What makes you think God hates you?" I asked.

"I'm pathetic, evil, and God hates me," he now shouted. I could feel his breath. He pulled hard on the chair and sat down, slamming its legs on the concrete floor.. "Hates me, hates me, hates me!"

We don't know what God thinks, I thought. We don't even know what God is.

I asked him why he wanted to see a minister.

He started sobbing, repeating again that God hates him, leaning over the table, shaking his head from side to side. After a pause, he looked me in the eye and asked, now in a soft voice: "Why? Why am I so evil? How could God let this happen to me? Why does God hate me so?"

I was unsure of where to go with him, so I said "Let's have a prayer to start this off."

I prayed, maybe not the way many do, not long orations that are supposed to be spellbinding, that assume that the divine has the capacity to keep up with every detail of everyone's life, therefore what's transpiring is already known. My prayer was something like, if it be your will, help this guy out, and show him the love you are reputed to show to all life infinitely, through the grace that helps us find a way to flourish. I liked the idea that something spiritually compassionate and wise was involved in the flourishing of life, human life included. Liked it, felt it was present, but also wondered whether it was a delusion.

I decided to consider the young man unhinged, irretrievably damaged. Maybe the best I could do was show him a human who listened, even though his fate was obvious. I figured he might see more ministers if this was what he needed while in prison, and that I was just one, maybe the first. I could be the last, too, though.

He wasn't going to get away with murder, this was certain. And wherever he may be now, as I write this, is a mystery to me. If alive, he no doubt still is confined, most likely in New York state. New York had no death penalty when he was convicted. Since his case, a death penalty had been enacted into law but a court declared it to violate the state's constitution, so in effect there is a moratorium on capital punishment. He didn't face execution. For him, it was life-imprisonment.

You're in for it, man, I thought, as he sat across from me. I let him voice what he opened with, repeating that God hated him, and asking why was it his destiny to end up the way he did. He wanted an answer I couldn't provide. "Make the best of it," I finally counseled weakly. I signaled to the guard that I was ready to leave, and we parted.

In writing this episode and those that follow, I want to note that I'm changing the facts a little and using pseudonyms in place of names. My choice. Some whom I've met I only learned their first names. Others faced additional charges and imprisonment in another state and are inordinately difficult to trace. Others I've tried to find but failed. Anyway, I think the essence here is the story, not the names. I'll be true to who I understood the people to be.

I'm also going to be true to what I am, a skeptical person who blanched when someone called me "Pastor Fred." Or even, "Doctor Easton." The bishop who ordained me even called me a "prophet" at that moment. Was I ordained to be a "prophet" after so much grief in the process of approval of my ordination because of my progressive theological stance, as one who sees biblical texts as political,   liturgical, often mythical literature with indirect links at times to historical actuality? A prophet. I hardly thought so. Nice touch, though.

I should stop doing all this altogether, I had thought after Neal and I parted, figuring what I had to offer was too minimal. Stop doing the whole thing, the prison ministry, serving a church. But a minister engaged in full-time jail ministry who considered me a colleague phoned and asked me to handle another "client" for him. He labeled those he encountered in the county jail his clients. He was deeply into it.

I reluctantly said yes.

"The guy is a biker, accused with another one of killing a construction contractor during a robbery," the Rev. Allen Roberts said, also known as Pastor Al. "Big guy. I've been meeting with him. I think he's been through a conversion experience. I'd like you to check it out."

"Are you going to set it up?" I asked. I read about the case in the newspaper.

"It's already set up," he said. "For me. But I can't make it. Personal thing. I told the jail people I'd ask you. You're on their list. They said it would be okay."

"When?" I asked. Maybe I had a conflict.

"Tomorrow, 3 p.m.," he answered. I didn't.

Answer the call, I thought ironically.

The jail entry routine was similar to what one can see on TV:

Identify yourself and why you're there. Guard calls someone for verification, looks you over. Then, empty your pockets, put the stuff in a bag, give it to the guard, who labels it. Feel the pat down. The guard opens the first barred door electronically: Step inside. The first door closes. The second barred door opens. Walk through the opening. The second door shuts with a clank. Look at the video cameras blankly. Listen to the metallic chunks of sound echo through the entryway and the hallway. This sound could be the genesis for the pop musical style "heavy metal," I thought one time. I wondered wryly how those sounds would play during a church service. I also thought about Jerry Jeff Walker's jail song, "Mr. Bojangles," who jumped so high in his cell, jumped so high, then he lightly touched down. Would that play, as well?

Randy Bryce the biker was big, as Roberts described, and towered over me. He looked about six-foot-five, was muscular, blue-eyed, with long stringy blond hair and no tattoos. That was odd, I thought. No marks. The room we sat in was a larger one, just two chairs. We weren't locked in. A guard sat outside, facing us. I was supposed to get up, open the door and leave if there was trouble. The door was to my side. The big biker, I learned, faced another homicide charge as well in Virginia. So that would be at least two he had pending.

Officials here charged Bryce and his co-accused with pistol-whipping the construction contractor, who died from the blows. Bryce's court-appointed attorney aimed to get a second-degree murder charge reduced to manslaughter if a plea of innocence failed. Neither of the two confessed, nor was it clear who struck the victim, both their finger prints were on the pistol the police retrieved, a .45-caliber semi-automatic. Each of the accused said they had no idea who the assailant was and both denied it was him.

"We found the pistol there," Bryce was recorded to have told police. "He was dead when we got there. We were just there because he wanted to meet with us."

News reports indicated that both had prison records from assault and robbery convictions but apparently reporters were yet unaware that Bryce was wanted in a Virginia homicide. The news reports suggested that the pair conspired to confuse the case and sought separate trials to make prosecution difficult. It was also reported that they were caught because the victim was able to call police the night of the homicide after he heard someone break into his business building, where he had stayed late that evening. The two surrendered without incident when police arrived. On them police found several thousand dollars in cash. Quite a pattern, I thought.

I looked at Bryce. He had a bible with him. He studied me for a moment, then held up the bible.

"It's mine," he said. "As you can see, it's used. By me."

He asked me my name.

"Fred," I said.

"Pastor Fred," he said. I blanched. "They got it all wrong."

"And. This ain't no jailhouse conversion," he said emphatically.

Got it all wrong, I mused. Probably not.

"You're in a biker gang, right?" I asked. "How come no tattoos?"

The question surprised Bryce. He looked at me as if to say, what's up with you?

"Blood poisoning," he said. "I don't want it."

"I thought you'd come up with a biblical reason," I said. "Or something like, 'My body is a temple of the lord.'"

He looked at me again and held the gaze.

"So, why are you seeing Allen Roberts? Or a minister?," I asked. "From what you're suggesting with the bible there, seems like you got your faith in place. What do you want from us? A ticket out?"

"Ain't you something?" Bryce said. "Quick on the trigger. You guys don't have that kind of pull."

"You're right on that score," I said. "So, what are we doing here, a bible study? Is it that you want me to affirm to your accusers that you are indeed remorseful and on a path to redemption and that I could testify to this after our little get-together?"

He stood up slowly, angry. The guard outside moved toward the door. So did Bryce. He snapped his fingers at the guard.

"I'm through with you," he said. "Tell Roberts I only want to see him. When he comes, I'll tell him you're useless."

Okay, that was quick. I messed up on the compassionate part, I thought. But no matter, I sensed he wasn't genuine. Plus, he seemed very used to getting his way. I decided to stick with my first impression that he was playing a con game.

Soon after, a jury convicted Bryce and his companion, Kevin Darby, of unintentional manslaughter, but Bryce's sentence was put on hold. Virginia police ferried him to their state, where he was convicted again, this time of second-degree murder in the slaying of a woman biker and was sentenced to serve 45 years in Mecklenburg State Prison. Afterward, if released, he'd be returned to New York to serve his sentence in the death of the contractor. Some time later, I wrote him to see how he and his faith were holding up. He didn't answer.

Meantime, changes were in store for me. The bishop and her cabinet of district superintendents moved me to another church some distance from the county jail, a church in a holy mess because of increasingly aggravated confrontations with a woman pastor and divisions among the congregation members. "Calm the waters," I was told. "Calm them," I thought. "I have a reputation for troubling them."

This church was near the ancient Auburn maximum security prison, euphemistically called a "correctional facility," the second oldest prison in the state and reflecting its age. It was overcrowded with an undersized dusty small yard, a difficult place to serve time. Some friends asked if I'd like to share in biweekly bible studies with some of the prisoners, most of whom were in for life for homicide. "In for life," I mused. I agreed. I had never been inside a maximum security prison and wondered what lifers thought facing that fate, permanently inside.

I need to say that I didn't then, and especially now don't live in a vacuum consisting of churches and prisons. There's much more to it. I'm married, my spouse is social policy analyst and consultant, and we together have organized human-rights delegations to people struggling in the so-called underdeveloped world, particularly in Latin American and the Mideast. Ultimately, on those trips, the best we could do is offer a brief presence of solidarity, a sense that some folks from another part of the planet cared. Occasionally, we'd also provide some needed resources. These weren't mission trips. We had three stated goals: one, to introduce others in our country to the situations of those living in such straits; two, to offer ourselves as international witnesses who would tell others what we encountered. The third was to accompany some who were in danger. There was a fourth for me. I wanted to experience first-hand the impact of this kind of human oppression. It was a theological motive.

Helena and I were both divorced when we met, each with an adult child who was fairing well and with one adopted child, now an adult, who wasn't. Once we needed counseling and it helped. Now, we're tight.

I need to say, too, that I've been in jail twice, once in a hovel of a place in South Carolina, an overcrowded cell with a plugged toilet, slime on the floor and no place to sleep, there several days for involvement in a street brawl while in the military. Eventually, I was tried and given a suspended 60-day jail sentence for accidentally punching a plain clothes policeman, plus busted two grades by the paratrooper battalion I was part of when I returned to base. The second time, it was following an antiwar protest for refusing to leave an area officials decided needed to be vacated. In that case, I spent two days inside, bailed out, pleaded guilty, and paid a fine. So, for what it's worth, I've got a little notion of what it's like to be confined to a jail cell, to be under armed guard. Both penalties were misdemeanors. Plus I was blessed with the additional penalty of the lumps from the beating South Carolina police enjoyed inflicting. I still feel them inside. One neat little trick of theirs I particularly recall. Three guards picked me up, stretched me out horizontally and ran my head along jail cell bars, like a kid who runs a stick along a picket fence.

So, back to the main story, if it is the main story.

The Auburn prison ministry bible study was a monthly gathering in a chapel close to pay phones prisoners could use, as well as a library where some would research law books to draft appeals of their convictions. The bible study, for a few who attended, was a break from prison routine. Others apparently felt they'd gone through a conversion. We, on the team, made it informal and interactive. One prisoner was called "The Minister," a tall, thin African-American with a high voice who liked to expound in a Black Church preacherly style.

This obviously was a Christian setting compared to those who came to meet with Jewish prisoners. Another prison religious group also made its presence felt behind Auburn's walls, Black Muslims, whose members intimidated those in the group I was part of, especially targeting two lifers I met who paired up to seek converts. These two were among four white men in the group. Attending as well were three African-Americans and three Latinos, two who were native Dominicans and one a Venezuelan. Another Latino from Cuba attended when he wasn't in trouble for violating prison rules. Most were convicted of murder and sentenced to life. One apparently was wrongly convicted, according to others, and his case was going through appeal.

I wondered if Jimmy Neal was serving time here. But no one in our group knew of him.

Four things stick in my mind from these monthly gatherings.

One is the soap-carvings of the head of Jesus a Dominican gave me. Because they were technically contraband, I wasn't allowed to take them out of the prison. But they've been in my possession since that day. This man, Angel, was serving life imprisonment for a homicide during an armed robbery in New York City.

Another is an encounter with a man who wouldn't exactly say what his crime was but it was evident that he had enormous remorse for what I surmised was the rape and murder of a child. He understood his tendency and considered prison the best way to avoid committing a similar crime, so he was somewhat settled into this habitat. He said he prayed often for forgiveness and asked me if I thought he would be. I answered that repentance and forgiveness were very much a part of Christian teaching.

The third is conversations I had with the two men who teamed up to bring what they felt was a faith message to other prisoners, even in the face of rebuke and hostility. They considered themselves missionaries. Both were also convicted of homicide during armed robberies and had heavily researched the library's law books for avenues of appeal.

One day one asked me:

"Do you think God will look favorably upon what we're doing here and help us find a way to be free of this place? I pray for that."

I answered:

"This may be your calling. As an intimate of the prison, it may well be the place where you are supposed to carry out your ministry. As insiders. For life. Can you embrace that?"

He was disturbed my answer. So was I, even though it seemed theologically sound from my point of view. Soon after, I decided not to continue this work. I informed members of the team that I was through and said farewell to the prisoners.

In line with that, is the fourth thing that came to mind. I then fully realized that the robes of a clergy person I wore didn't fit. Not in the prison, not in the church.

It was clear that I had too many issues with church doctrine, with its teachings, especially those embraced by the evangelical wing of my denomination, with the understanding of the bible as divinely wrought, and with the interpretations of what the message of the man Jesus Christ was. I saw this message as radical, calling upon people of his time and perhaps people of the future to liberate the captives, free the oppressed, bring aid to the poor, and to ensure that goods and services be balanced so that all human may flourish; basically as a call for peace with justice. This is what struck me as "holy."

Among episodes while serving a church that brought my realization home was one that stood out. It involved two human rights trips I organized to Palestine and Israel, especially visiting Palestinian

Christians who felt the same heavy hand of Israeli policy that Muslims did, one that resulted in another kind of imprisonment for them and passages through military checkpoints as well as constant confrontations from Israeli soldiers.

I had persuaded the congregation I served at the time to provide resources for kids attending a school operated by Palestinian Christians who were basically guided by what is known as liberation theology, somewhat along the lines of what I understood to be the mission of the man Jesus. I also understood it as prison ministry of a different kind, an action against an unjust incarceration of a people who had their legal rights to land willfully overturned and themselves displaced forcibly and brutally as well as their homes and goods destroyed. I saw the destroyed and damaged homes helicopter-gunship missiles and bulldozers had blasted and the evidence that the missiles the gunships used were United States issued. I also saw the damage inflicted on a Christian orphanage by Israeli thanks that had rammed the building.

Addressing what I witnessed in the church I served, I created a division. The final straw followed the 9/11 terrorist attack on the World Trade Center in New York City said to have been executed by Al Qaeda Islamic fundamentalists. Just a few days earlier, I had returned from my second Mideast trip. When I offered photos of young Palestinian school students during a church service shortly after the attack, a congregation member called them "the children of Osama bin Laden." Others laughed. That was too much. The gap between me and those who thought that way was clearly unbridgeable. I decided to retire. "Don't call me Pastor Fred," I finally said aloud. I felt I too was a prisoner of an institution that kept evidencing that it was far from what I understood theology to mean. I knew I'd be unable to change what I felt was wrong. I was clearheaded enough to realize that.

Now, looking back, I decided maybe writing about it might offer the remote possibility that some understanding might occur. On the other hand, I doubt this will happen. Still, it feels right to put these words on a page.

I suppose I need to add an epilogue about what I'm doing now. One, obviously, is writing. Helena and I live in an A-frame dwelling on the Cumberland Plateau in Tennessee with our pets. She had successfully set herself up as a consultant and now does pretty well so we survive from her income and my retirement fixed income. I've also joined the huge community of internet bloggers, writing about social and theological issues, but few people read my blog. Maybe that will change, maybe not. Our kids visit frequently also, even our troubled adopted child, a good thing. We also maintain an organic garden for some food. Basically, though, I'm now a recluse. I prefer it that way. I did my part.

THE POEMS

Alien Bones

Myths or truths
the story is this
She, Clementine, from Ireland
flees the famine, steerage on the sea
to Prince Edward Island
labeled low class
but able, able to cook woodcutters meals
toiling for lumber barons
No sables for her.

He, first mate and artist
Wilhelm, shipping from Hamburg
painting seascapes as part of his sailor's fate
to sail the lumber to his homeland, to Deutschland
No white ties for him.

They meet, he jumps ship
they slip southward on an underground trail
or by hidden sail
Who now knows, knows these aliens again
No open door for them.

From the stove of the lumber camp
from the meals in the galley
they enter the alleys
of Hells Kitchen
Kitchen, illegal melting pot
What, no papers? Here. A price
A solution for them.

Bones from Ireland
Bones from Deutschland
Alien bones that sailed
and prevailed a little
Bones now buried,
buried somewhere in Long Island
Faded memories for them

The Automat

I took the bus, then the El
then the subway
under the spell of the city
I'm nine at the time

Inside, through the window
little cubicles on display
coin in a slot opens a door
little brown bean pot
I put on my automat tray

On the table
even in boyhood I'm not confused
by a newspaper's views from Alamogordo
mushroom cloud that wouldn't go away

Thick cup by a sign
Inside someone flipped
a menthol stub
lipstick on the tip
and so it's mine.

Billboard smoke rings on Times Square
from Willie the Penguin
whose voice dubbed there
lures me to
"Smoke Kools. Smoke Kools"

Mushroom clouds from the desert
Wisps of steam from sidewalk grates

And the rumble below
The tumble within
resemble my city childhood.

The Smile Hasn't Left

The smile hasn't left
though that schoolyard day
you Jack Tommy Alfred
bled me a little
Ganging up holding me down
to play a game of shoe
Track shoe on my body
Piling on the little nicks
The spikes you thought
would make me wince
and cry

And why the smile still
to this day
decades since?
It's a wry notion
wrought when I heard that you
Jack and Alfred
died later on
downtown
in a shootout with police
Failed holdup that stuck
you Tommy in prison
still in your teens
caught and brought up short

No Wind, No Keel

No wind, no keel
a hole in the sail trailing
Satellite phone, no signal
Waves higher than the mast
Holding on to the rudder
Holding on ...
Holding fast to the past
The bearings, recollections, flotations
life jackets,
as the sun sets

Tick Tock

Wasted a minute
Wait a minute
Give me a minute

Can we take back that last minute
when 15,000 children died
in our world
due to poverty
That yesterday when …
Last year, when
When?

Say.
You got a minute?

Opening the Gate -- Wes Rehberg

Openng the Gate   --   Wes Rehberg

ABOUT THE AUTHOR

Wes Rehberg is a long-time social justice activist, writer and has also recently worked in video art and documentary filmmaking. He has a Ph.D. in philosophy, interpretation and culture from Binghamton University. He recently began fiction and poetry writing as well and has begun publishing in these areas. Wes is married to artist and social policy analyst Eileen Rehberg, who has worked with him on several projects. Their home page is www.wildclearing.com -- Wes was also a print journalist for 22 years with newspapers in NJ and NY. He has four children, Stacey, John, Vivian and Scott, and since his marriage to Eileen, shares in the families of her two children, Luke and Chris Robertson. He and Eileen currently live in Chattanooga, Tennessee and have a little mountain cabin retreat in upstate New York.